S0-AWA-547

This book belongs to:

Samantha

Copyright © 1991, 1992, 1993, 1995 by Shogo Hirata. Originally published by Joie, Inc.
Copyright © 1995 Modern Publishing, a division of Unisystems, Inc.

Formerly published as Fun-To-Read™ Fairy Tales. ® Honey Bear Books is a trademark owned by
Honey Bear Productions, Inc., and is registered in the U.S. Patent and Trademark Office.
All Rights Reserved.
No part of this book may be reproduced or copied in any format without
written permission from the publisher.

Snow White
and other Favorite Tales

Modern Publishing
A Division of Unisystems, Inc.
New York, New York 10022
Printed in Italy

Contents

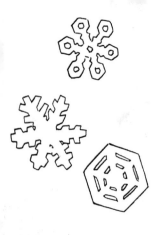

Once in a far away land, a king and queen had a lovely baby daughter. She was born on a snowy day, and the queen said, "Our daughter is as beautiful and wonderful as each falling snowflake. We shall name her Snow White."

Sadly, the queen died while Snow White was quite young. Some years later, the king decided to marry again. He introduced Snow White to his new wife. "I will be your stepmother, Snow White," the woman said. "I'm sure you and I will get along quite well." She laughed wickedly. Snow White shivered.

The new queen was a powerful magician. She was evil and vain as well. Everyday she would ask her magical mirror, "Looking glass upon the wall, who is fairest of us all?"

"You are the fairest," the mirror would answer, and the queen would smile.

But when the queen came to live with the king and Snow White, the mirror's answer changed.

"Who is the fairest in all the kingdom?" the queen asked her mirror.

"Snow White is the fairest!" the mirror answered.

As Snow White's lovely face appeared in the magical mirror, the queen flew into a rage.

"She will not be the fairest in the kingdom for long!" vowed the queen, and she called for a huntsman. "Take my stepdaughter far into the woods until she is outside of the kingdom. Then leave her there," she told the huntsman. The huntsman tried to protest, but the queen insisted, "Do as I say or I'll have your head and your wife's, too. You are not to tell anyone about this!"

The huntsman did as the queen ordered and left Snow White in the woods, unable to find her way home.

After much wandering, Snow White came upon a small cottage. She knocked on the door, but no one answered. Snow White was cold and tired, so she let herself in.

Once inside, Snow White fell sound asleep. She didn't hear the owners of the cottage come home.

Seven dwarfs lived in the cottage. They were surprised to find Snow White when they came home from their long day's work.

Snow White woke when she heard the stamping of their heavy boots. After a moment's fright she saw their gentle smiles and knew she was among friends. Snow White told the dwarfs all about her evil stepmother.

"Please, stay here with us!" the dwarfs cheered.

"Thank you! I will take good care of all of you," Snow White promised.

Snow White loved taking care of the dwarfs and their home.

She didn't know, however, that the huntsman had not taken her far enough into the woods and that she was still within her father's kingdom. But the queen knew. The mirror still said Snow White was the fairest in the kingdom and the queen was furious. She decided to get rid of Snow White once and for all.

With her magical powers, the queen put an evil spell on a silk ribbon. Then she disguised herself as an old peddler and went to the dwarfs' cottage, where she tricked Snow White into buying the ribbon.

No sooner had Snow White tried on the ribbon than she fell to the floor in a deep sleep.

Luckily, the dwarfs took the ribbon off as soon as they found her, and Snow White woke up.

"You must be more careful of strangers," the dwarfs scolded.

But when the queen again came in disguise, Snow White forgot the dwarfs' warning and accepted an apple.

The apple was poisoned, and after one bite, Snow White fell to the ground.

This time the dwarfs did not know how to save
their beloved friend. It appeared Snow White would
never wake again.

Sadly, the dwarfs placed Snow White in a beautiful glass box filled with white roses. They carried her to a peaceful spot in the forest. Just as they were saying good-bye, a prince on a fine white horse stopped to see what was happening.

The prince gazed at Snow White and fell in love with her. How he wished she could be his bride. Then he bent down and kissed her gently.

As he did so, Snow White's eyes began to flutter and she woke from her deep sleep. The dwarfs danced and sang as Snow White told the prince what happened. He proposed marriage, and Snow White happily accepted.

The prince couldn't wait to tell his father, the king, that Snow White was to become his bride.

The dwarfs followed Snow White and her prince to the edge of the forest. They were going to miss their friend. Snow White smiled and promised to come back and visit them often. She thanked the seven dwarfs for all their love and kindness.

Then Snow White and the prince rode off together.

Long ago and far away, there was a widower who had a young daughter named Ella.

One day, the widower introduced Ella to a lady with two daughters. "This lady and I are to be married tomorrow. She will be your stepmother. And these are your stepsisters, Hilda and Gilda," said Ella's father. "Sadly, I must leave on a long trip right after the wedding."

Ella was very surprised. But she was so sweet and good she welcomed her new family. "I shall see to whatever they need, Father," Ella promised.

Ella worked hard to make everyone happy. Her stepmother always had a chore for Ella. As for Hilda and Gilda, they played, rested and ate sweets all day.

"My daughters are too delicate for common housework," said Ella's stepmother. "They are fine young ladies, sure to marry royalty."

Ella worked long into the night, sitting down to a plain supper many hours after everyone else had gone to bed.

Even though Ella did all she could to please her
stepsisters, they often teased her cruelly.

One day, Hilda said to Gilda, "Look at her
gathering cinders from the fireplace. Let's call
her Cinderella!"

That afternoon, a royal messenger came to the
door with an invitation to the prince's ball.
"Whatever shall we wear?" cried Gilda.

Hilda, Gilda and their mother dressed in their finest clothes.

"What shall I wear?" asked Cinderella.

"You were not invited!" cried her stepmother.

In truth, Cinderella had been invited, but her stepmother knew that if Cinderella went to the ball, the prince would never look at Hilda or Gilda, who were somewhat homely and not very nice.

Cinderella did not trust her stepmother's word. She went to check the invitation, but found it had already been burned in the fire.

That night, Cinderella sat in her room, sadly thinking about the ball. "How I wish I could go," she sighed.

"And so you shall!" said a voice. To Cinderella's amazement a fairy appeared from out of nowhere.

"I am your Fairy Godmother," said the fairy. "I've come to grant your wish."

She led Cinderella out into the
yard. With a wave of her wand,
the fairy changed a pumpkin into
a golden coach and four white
mice into fine white horses.
Two salamanders became handsome
coachmen.

"That's wonderful," Cinderella
gasped. "But Fairy Godmother, I
have nothing to wear."

The fairy smiled and waved her
wand once more.

Cinderella looked down and found herself wearing a beautiful ball gown. There were jewels in her hair, and on her feet were a pair of tiny glass dancing slippers. "Thank you, Fairy Godmother!" Cinderella cried.

"You must leave the ball before midnight!" the fairy warned. "The magic will last only until then!"

Cinderella promised she would, and off she went to the ball.

Everyone at the ball noticed how the prince gazed at the beautiful stranger and how he danced with no one else for the rest of the night. Nobody knew it was Cinderella.

Suddenly, the clock struck twelve!

Cinderella ran from the palace as fast as she could. The prince followed, but Cinderella disappeared into the night before he could catch up to her.

In her haste, Cinderella lost one of her glass
slippers. The prince found it and picked it up.
Cradling the tiny shoe in his hands, he said, "If I must
search the kingdom ten times over, I will find the
beautiful lady who fits into this slipper.

When I do, I will marry her, for she is the most
wonderful maiden I have ever met!"

The next day, the search for the prince's true love began. Every home in the kingdom was visited…and every maiden, including Hilda and Gilda, tried to squeeze her foot into the glass slipper. The shoe was so tiny, no one's foot could fit inside.

As the prince's men were leaving Cinderella's home, they saw her working in the garden.

"What about her?" asked one of the men.

"Who? Cinderella? Why, she's just a common servant," lied her stepmother. "Surely, you don't mean to have her try. She didn't even attend the ball!"

The prince's men insisted that Cinderella try on the slipper.

Much to everyone's surprise it fit perfectly.

While Hilda, Gilda and her stepmother shrieked in outrage, Cinderella was led out of the house and away to the castle.

There she met her handsome prince. He was so happy to have found his true love once again.

On the very next day Cinderella and the prince were married, and lived happily ever after.

A very long time ago, there lived a king and a queen who had everything they wanted, except a child of their own. "Oh, how wonderful it would be to hear the joyous laughter of a child's voice in the palace," sighed the queen.

"Yes, my dear," said the king, who only wanted to make his wife happy. Many years would pass before their wish would come true.

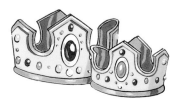

Then, one glorious day the king and queen were blessed with a beautiful baby daughter!

To celebrate, all the fairies of the kingdom were invited to a feast—all but one. There was no room at the table for her. One by one the fairies gave the little princess a special gift.

"She will be a happy child," said the first.

"She will be kind...graceful... helpful...loyal...caring," said the others in turn.

Before the last fairy could give her gift, the doors blew open and the fairy who hadn't been invited stormed into the room.

"Why wasn't I invited to the feast? I, too, have a special gift for your precious princess," she screamed, waving her skull-topped wand.

"When she is sixteen years old, she will prick her finger on a spinning wheel and die!" Then the wicked fairy vanished from the palace.

The king and queen were horrified. They couldn't believe that something like this could ever happen.

63

Fortunately, the last fairy still had to give the baby a gift. "Should ever this child prick her finger," said the fairy, "she will not die but will fall asleep for one hundred years or until she is awakened by a kiss of true love."

The very next day, the king ordered all the
spinning wheels in the land to be burned. The
king's soldiers quickly carried out his orders.

When the princess was sixteen years old, she came upon a staircase leading to a tower in the castle. She climbed higher and higher up the stone stairs, and at the top she saw a woman at a large spinning wheel.

"What a wonderful wheel you have!" the princess exclaimed.

"Come closer and see," invited the woman.

"What is this?" the princess asked touching the wheel's pointy needle. The moment she did so, she fell into a deep sleep.

"At last," shouted the woman, who was really the wicked fairy in disguise. She thought her long-ago curse of death had felled the young princess.

The king and queen were heartbroken to discover their lovely daughter in the death-like sleep that was to last a century.

When the good fairy discovered what had happened, she cast a spell over the entire palace. Everyone quickly fell into a deep sleep. No one would awaken until the princess did.

From that day on, many young men attempted to end the enchantment and to find the princess. They all perished in the briars that grew thicker year in and year out around the palace.

Many years later, a young prince who was the bravest, kindest, and wisest of them all heard of the strange curse over the palace and of the sleeping beauty within. He was determined to save her.

With sword and shield in hand, he tried valiantly to slash his way through the thick briars and thorns. But his sword was no match for the monstrous hedges.

Then, the good fairy appeared and gave him the king's own mighty sword. With it, the courageous prince was victorious!

Watching in her crystal ball, the wicked fairy became enraged when she saw that the prince had reached the tower door.

To thwart him, she summoned her most ferocious dragon. The prince blocked the dragon's flames with his shield and threw his powerful sword—striking the dragon dead.

When he reached the sleeping princess, the prince was over-whelmed by his love for her. She looked so lovely and peaceful as she slept. He knelt down and sweetly kissed her. His gentle kiss of true love woke the princess at last.

Finally, the evil spell had been broken. The entire palace soon came back to life. The king and queen awoke and embraced the happy couple. All the knights, the ladies, and servants rejoiced. Moments later, outside the palace, the thick briar also disappeared.

The princess and prince were married on the very next day. Of course, all the fairies were invited to the festivities—all except the wicked one!

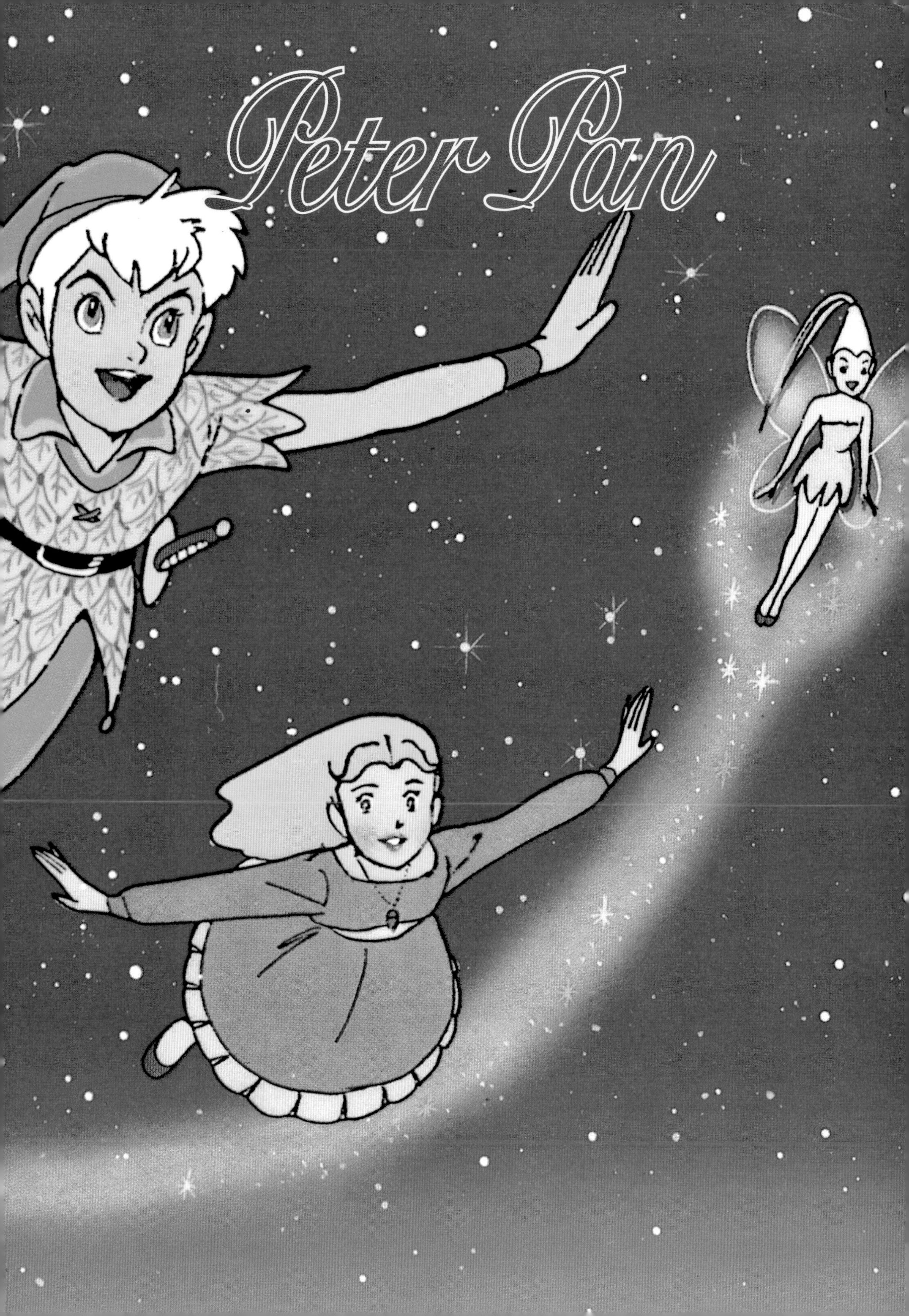
Peter Pan

A long time ago, there was a family named Darling. One night, Mr. and Mrs. Darling went to a party, leaving their children—Wendy, John, and Michael—in the care of their family dog, Nana.

"Hurry, Dear, or we'll be late," called out Mr. Darling.

"Oh, how I wish I wasn't going to a party tonight," sighed Mrs. Darling as she put on her coat. "I want to stay home with the children."

Later, while Wendy was telling her brothers a bedtime story, a strange boy dressed in green jumped into the room. A tiny glowing fairy flew in beside him. Nana didn't know the strangers, so she leaped up to catch the boy but caught his shadow instead.

"Ouch!" the boy shrieked. The shadow ripped off the boy's shoes and was held fast by Nana's paw.

"Who are you?" asked Wendy.

"I am Peter Pan, and this fairy is Tinker Bell," the boy exclaimed. "Now give me back my shadow!"

Wendy sewed Peter's shadow back on his shoes. "We are from a place called Neverland," Peter explained to the Darling children. "We live there with the Lost Boys who have run away from their parents."

"What are you doing here?" Wendy asked.

"Tinker Bell and I often listen at the window to your storytelling."

Peter thanked Wendy for reuniting him with his shadow, and gave her an acorn button which she put on a chain and wore around her neck.

"Come with me to Neverland!" Peter said. "I will sprinkle you with fairy dust so you can fly! You can tell me and the Lost Boys stories every night!"

Wendy, Michael and John were eager to go to Neverland with Peter Pan and Tinker Bell. With a sprinkling of fairy dust, they flew off with Peter. As they neared the island, a great blast shook the Neverland sky.

"It's the pirates, led by Hook!" cried Peter. "They are shooting at us!"

"Who is Hook?" cried John.

"He is the captain of the pirates!" shouted Peter. "He hates me because I cut off his hand and a crocodile snapped it up. Now the captain wears an iron hook where his hand used to be!"

Just then, the winds arose and split up the group. Peter and Tinker Bell were carried one way, John and Michael another, and Wendy another.

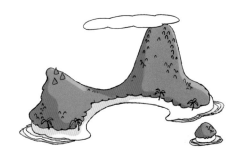

"Go after Wendy, Tinker Bell!"
Peter exclaimed.

Tinker Bell found Wendy flying
near the home of the Lost Boys.

One of the boys shot an arrow
and Wendy fell to the ground.

But the acorn button stopped the
arrow from harming Wendy. Peter's
gift had saved her life.

Wendy took care of the Lost Boys. She told them stories and tucked them in at night.

One day, Peter, Wendy and the boys were playing on the rocks in the Mermaids' Lagoon. They saw Tiger Lily, an Indian princess, being kidnapped by pirates. Peter rushed to rescue her.

Captain Hook tried to capture Peter, too, but
when the crocodile suddenly appeared, Captain
Hook ran away. Hook was too afraid of the crocodile
to chase after Peter and Tiger Lily.

That night, the Indians had a dance to celebrate Tiger Lily's rescue. Wendy went home early to watch over the boys.

As the boys slept, Wendy baked a cake for Peter, and left a note telling him to have a piece when he got home.

Suddenly, Captain Hook and the pirates burst
into the room, capturing Wendy and the boys!

Captain Hook poured poison over the cake
Wendy left for Peter. Then the pirates took their
prisoners back to the ship.

Luckily, Tinker Bell saw what Hook had done.
When Peter came home, Tinker Bell knocked the
cake on the floor before Peter had a chance to eat it.
    She told Peter what had happened, and they
set off for the pirate ship.

Peter Pan crept aboard the ship and hid in the cabin below. Then he began to make strange sounds. He knew cowardly Hook would send the prisoners to investigate.

Once the boys were in the cabin, Peter gathered them together to fight against the evil pirates.

Peter fought with Hook. When Hook fell overboard—right into the jaws of the crocodile—everyone cheered.

Wendy, John and Michael decided it was time for them to return home.

With a sprinkle of fairy dust the ship sailed high in the sky with everyone aboard. When they neared the Darling house, Peter Pan and Tinker Bell flew with Wendy, and her brothers to the nursery window.

Wendy, John and Michael waved to Peter Pan, Tinker Bell and the Lost Boys as they flew off to Neverland.

"Good-bye! Good-bye!" the children said.

Then they turned to hug Nana, and their parents, who were ever so happy the children had come home.

A long time ago, there was a lonely woman, who wanted more than anything in the world to have a baby. So, she went to visit a wise old fairy, who gave her a magic grain of barleycorn. The fairy told her to go home right away and plant it in a flowerpot.

As soon as the woman did, a beautiful flower immediately sprouted. It looked like a real tulip, but inside there was a lovely maiden no bigger than a thumb. Her mother called her Thumbelina.

Day in and day out, lovely Thumbelina
brought joy to her mother's heart. She sailed on a
roseleaf in a dishful of water singing happy songs.

But as Thumbelina slept in her walnut shell
bed, an old toad peered at her through the
open window.

"She would be a beautiful bride for my son,"
the toad said to himself.

In the middle of the night, the old toad carried Thumbelina off to the pond and placed her on a lily pad. The young toad croaked with glee and waited for his wedding day.

But all the fishes who lived in the pond knew Thumbelina was too beautiful a girl to marry the warty toad. So they nibbled at the lily roots and soon grateful Thumbelina was floating down the river toward an uncertain future!

On the way, Thumbelina met a friendly butterfly.

"Hold this vine and I'll pull you along," the delicate butterfly told Thumbelina.

"How nice it is to be away from the old toad and his son," Thumbelina thought.

Suddenly, Thumbelina was lifted off the lily pad by a great flying bug. He took Thumbelina above the river to his nest in the trees. His friends made fun of Thumbelina since she only had two arms and two legs and no wings at all. So the bug decided to let Thumbelina go.

But spring had turned into fall and then winter, and although Thumbelina was glad to have her freedom, she was lost in the forest with nowhere to live. The dry leaves that blew across the forest floor were not enough to keep Thumbelina warm, and she was very hungry and lonely.

She walked on and on until she came upon a cottage in the woods.

"Is anyone home?" Thumbelina asked softly.

A kindly country mouse opened the door and welcomed Thumbelina into her home. As the snow fell outside, Thumbelina was given a hearty meal by the warm fire.

"I'm glad for your company," Fieldmouse said. "And you can keep house for me in return for room and board."

Thumbelina was happy with the arrangement. She worked for Fieldmouse and enjoyed her company, too. But whenever she could, Thumbelina would go outside for the fresh air and sun, and she'd listen to the birds, oftentimes singing her lovely songs with them.

One evening a neighbor of
Fieldmouse's came to visit.

"This is Mr. Mole,"
announced Fieldmouse as she
introduced Thumbelina to her
nearsighted friend.

Fieldmouse had told
Thumbelina all about Mr. Mole.
"He's very rich and would make
a good husband," Fieldmouse
had said as they waited for him
to arrive.

Mr. Mole was pleased to meet
Thumbelina and allowed
Fieldmouse and Thumbelina to
walk through the underground
tunnel that he'd dug beneath the
two houses.

"Stay out of the dreadful sun
and cold," he suggested, since he
preferred to be underground in
the dark.

One day, with candle in hand, Thumbelina ventured down into the dark caves. To her surprise she found a bird lying on the ground. Her heart broke to see such a lovely creature lying dead, but as she laid her head upon Swallow's breast she heard its heart faintly beating.

Thumbelina lovingly brought Swallow food and water and covered him with a blanket to keep him warm. Soon Swallow was well again and thanked Thumbelina for being so kind.

"Come with me, Thumbelina, to another land where the sunshine is warm and birds sing all year long." But Thumbelina felt obligated to help Fieldmouse, who had been so kind to her.

Thumbelina waved goodbye to her feathered friend and missed him badly even before he was out of sight.

Fieldmouse convinced
Thumbelina that marrying Mr.
Mole was the best thing to do. With
no other prospects, Thumbelina
began preparing for her wedding.
Mr. Mole was looking forward to
welcoming Thumbelina to his dark
underground home.

On her wedding day, Thumbelina sat in the
sunshine and tried to sing a happy song, but there
were only tears in her eyes and sobs in her throat.

All the forest creatures gathered round to
cheer up Thumbelina. Then Swallow flew
down from high above and landed near his
dear friend Thumbelina.

Thumbelina told him about Mr. Mole.

"You saved my life, Thumbelina. Now come away with me to a far-off land where you can start again," said Swallow. Thumbelina agreed.

She flew with Swallow as he soared high into the sky above Fieldmouse's house and far, far away from Mr. Mole's underground home.

When they reached the
Kingdom of Flowers, Swallow told
Thumbelina to pick a flower to be
her new home. When she did, it
opened and out stepped a
handsome young man with wings
and a crown.

"Welcome to my kingdom," he
told Thumbelina. "I'm the King
of Flowers."

As Thumbelina looked
around she saw all the Flower
people fluttering around. The dainty
creatures welcomed Thumbelina
and she knew she'd found the
home she'd always wanted.

When the King asked Thumbelina to be his bride, Thumbelina accepted with joy. Then Swallow sang a happy song for the tiny couple.

The King gave Thumbelina a crown and wings so she'd be able to live happily ever after in the magical Kingdom of Flowers.

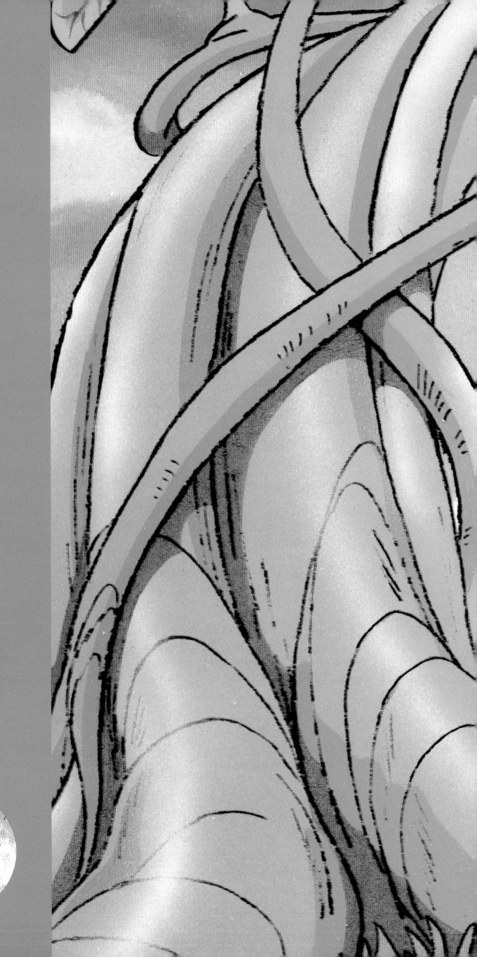

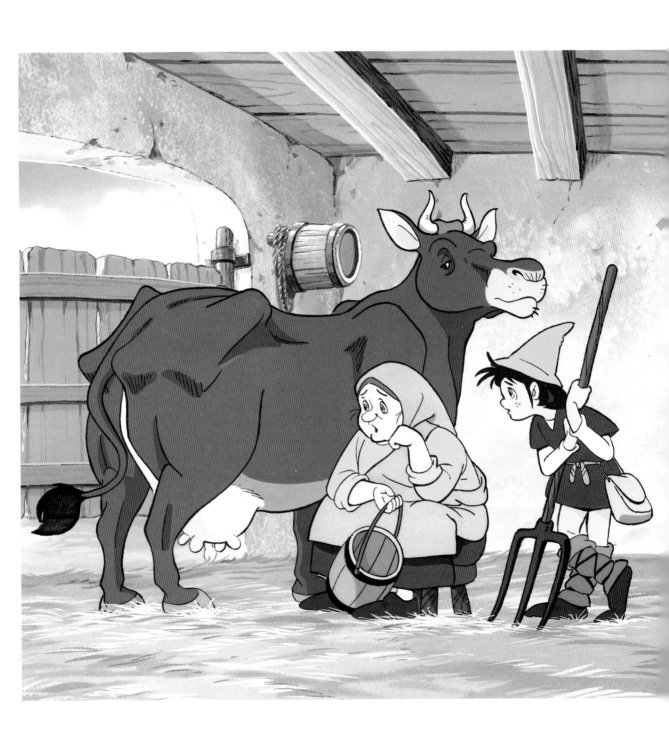

Jack and his mother were poor farmers who lived by selling their crops, until one day when there were no more crops to sell. All they had left of value was their cow, Buttercup.

"Take Buttercup to market today, and sell her," Jack's mother said sadly. "But be sure you get a good price—it's all the money we'll have in the world."

Jack roped Buttercup and took her to town. On the way he met a man sitting by the side of the road. The man offered to trade a magic bean for Buttercup.

Jack took the magic bean quickly, before the man could change his mind!

Later that afternoon Jack returned home,
skipping merrily. "Look what I got for Buttercup,"
he told his mother proudly. "It's a magic bean…"

"How could you be so foolish, child?" his mother
scolded. She threw the bean out the window.

Jack awoke at dawn the next day. When he looked out the window he saw that a tree had sprouted from the bean!

The stalk grew way up into the sky, far beyond the clouds, and passed the birds flying overhead. In fact, Jack couldn't see the top of the beanstalk, so he decided to climb it.

Holding on tightly, Jack climbed higher and higher until he could see the entire village below him...and above, he saw a castle floating in the clouds!

"Hello," Jack shouted as he reached the castle door. When it opened, Jack was amazed. A washerwoman stood before him but she was a giant!

"Oh good, a boy to do my work for me," she said. "Mind my master doesn't find you or he'll eat you for dinner."

Curiously, Jack followed her inside.

Moments later, the castle
shook under Jack's feet.

"Oh no, here comes the master,"
said the fearful washerwoman.
"You'd better hide." Jack ran
behind the bricks in the fireplace.

"Fee-fi-fo-fum,
I smell the blood of a runty one!
Be he live or be he dead,
his bones I'll grind to make my bread!"

A monstrous giant entered the
room and Jack trembled. "I smell
a boy," the giant yelled at the
washerwoman.

"There's no boy here, sir," she
said timidly.

"Better not be, or else. Bring
me my gold NOW," he commanded.

After counting his gold, the mean giant fell asleep. Jack crept up onto the table and ran off with a sack of coins for his mother.

"Look, Mother, we're rich," Jack said
happily. Then he told her about the beanstalk,
the enchanted castle and the ferocious giant.

But the gold was soon spent, so Jack climbed
the beanstalk again, hoping to find more of the
ogre's treasure.

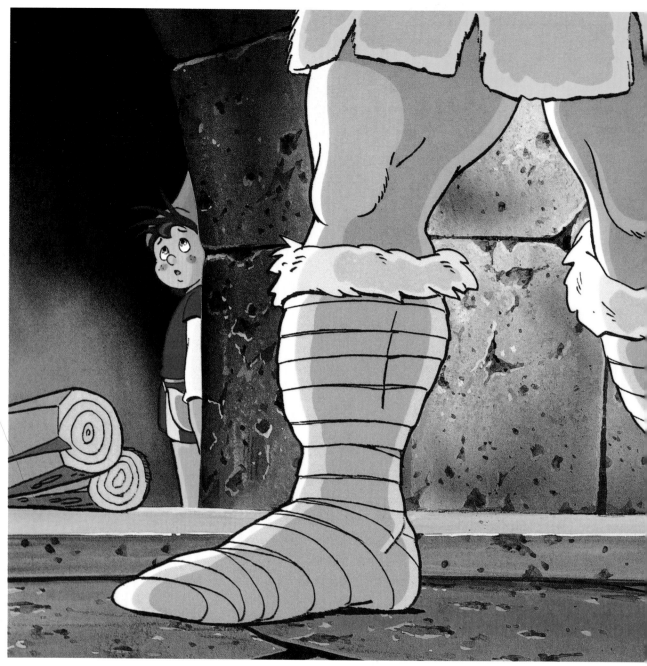

No sooner was Jack in the castle than he heard,
"Fee-fi-fo-fum,
I smell the blood of a runty one!
Be he live or be he dead,
his bones I'll grind to make my bread!"

Jack hid while the brute searched nearly everywhere.

146

"Bring me my hen NOW," demanded the
giant tyrant, of the washerwoman. Once again,
the giant sat at his table, this time with a
squawking hen upon it. To Jack's surprise he
saw the hen lay an egg of solid gold!

When the wretched giant fell asleep, Jack took the hen and hurried back down the beanstalk.

But when the hen died, Jack climbed way up the beanstalk to the castle yet again.

"Bring me my harp NOW," he heard the miserable giant order. The meek washerwoman brought a golden harp that told the giant the secrets of the universe.

When the beastly giant fell asleep, Jack crawled onto the table and grabbed the harp from within an inch of the monster's hand!

"Master, Master!" called out the harp as Jack ran away with it. "Help me! Help me!"

The giant woke and saw Jack taking the talking harp. Enraged, the giant chased Jack to the beanstalk. The giant waved his spiked bat furiously and narrowly missed Jack with every blow!

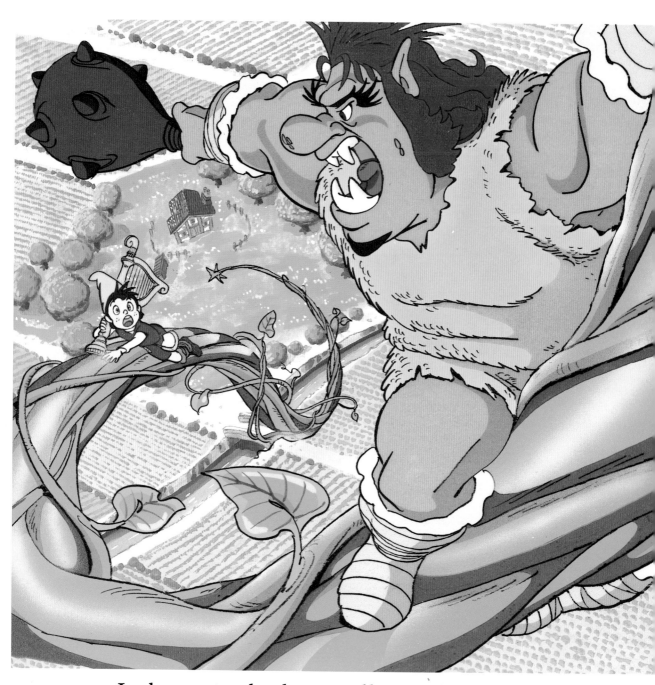

Jack ran to the beanstalk and began to climb down. The angry giant was right behind and getting closer.

"Mother, Mother, bring an axe!" shouted Jack as he reached the bottom of the beanstalk. His mother came running to save her son from the vicious giant.

Jack chopped through the stalk. He barely got out of the way before the giant crashed to the ground at his feet. The earth shook so from his landing that Jack was thrown up into the air and the giant fell into a deep hole, never to be seen again.

Jack and his mother became rich after selling the golden eggs. With the wise advice from the all-knowing harp, Jack and his mother would remain rich for the rest of their lives, and never want for anything again.